Once More ...

The Gaskitts!

First published 2003 by Walker Books Ltd
87 Vauxhall Walk, London SE11 5HJ

2 4 6 8 10 9 7 5 3 1

Text © 2003 Allan Ahlberg
Illustrations © 2003 Katharine McEwen

This book has been typeset in Stempel Schneidler,
Cafeteria, Tapioca and Kosmik

Printed in Italy

British Library Cataloguing in Publication Data:
a catalogue record for this book
is available from the British Library

ISBN 0-7445-9632-7

Allan Ahlberg

The Cat Who Got Carried Away

illustrated by

Katharine McEwen

WALKER BOOKS
AND SUBSIDIARIES
LONDON • BOSTON • SYDNEY

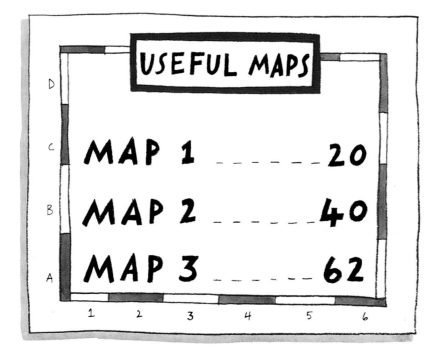

USEFUL MAPS

MAP 1 _____ 20

MAP 2 _____ 40

MAP 3 _____ 62

Contents

1 The Barking Pram 8

2 Fried Egg and Pineapple 13

3 Meet Mr Cruncher 22

4 Have You Seen This Hamster? 31

5 Honest Joe 42

6 The Great Escape 47

7 That Pram Again 53

8 Clever Randolph! 56

9 Running Like the Wind 64

10 The Final Timetable 73

11 Meanwhile... 76

Gaskitts Story

Mrs Gaskitt

hardly ever gets
out of bed.

Why is that?

And Horace –

poor Horace! – ends up ...
in a pet shop!

*£5?
I'm a bargain!*

£5

★★★ **Also Starring** ★★★
A rat named **Randolph,**
a guinea pig named **Maurice**
and a teacher named **Mrs Fritter**
(who sometimes falls over).

Not to mention a mysterious
gang of... But more of them later.

ON WITH THE STORY!

Chapter One
The Barking Pram

Early one evening the Gaskitts were at home sitting side by side on Mr and Mrs Gaskitt's bed. All except Mrs Gaskitt – she was in bed.

 Why is that? It's only half past seven.

Anyway, there they were drinking tea, eating biscuits and looking at the family photo album.

There was a photo of Gus and Gloria as babies,
a photo of Horace as a kitten and a photo of
Mr and Mrs Gaskitt … dancing.

"On our honeymoon,"

said Mr Gaskitt.

"But what about us?"

"Were we born then?"

the children cried.

"Not quite," said Mrs Gaskitt.

"We had the house to ourselves."

"Yes." Mr Gaskitt smiled.

"It was delightful."

(Gloria punched him.)

"I mean boring."

(And Gus hit him

with a pillow.)

Boring!
Boring!
Boring!

Meanwhile, Horace was outside

sitting on the garden wall

watching the world go by.

He saw a boy on a bike,

a boy on a skateboard,

a woman in a car

and, finally,

on the other side of the road,

a man absolutely *whizzing* along

with a really old pram.

And the strange thing was,

which Horace noticed,

the strange thing was, the pram ...

Woof, woof!

was barking.

Chapter Two
Fried Egg and Pineapple

The next morning

everybody got up.

Gus and Gloria got up

and went to school.

Mr Gaskitt got up

and went shopping.

Mrs Gaskitt got up, got the paper,

got the post,

got a cup of tea

and a *cream doughnut* ...

and went back to bed.

Goodness me!

Meanwhile, Horace was out on the wall again

hoping to see and hear that

mysterious pram.

Well, Horace never saw
the pram that time,
but Mr Gaskitt did.

He was in his car at the school crossing

and there it was, the same as before,

with the same man just *whizzing* along.

But not barking, though. Oh, no!

It was more like … squeaking,

Mr Gaskitt thought.

15

When Gus and Gloria got to school

they found that something

dreadful had happened.

Randolph – clever, lovable Randolph –

the class rat, had ("Squeak, squeak!") …

disappeared.

Oh yes, and Mrs Fritter,
while trying to find him,
had fallen out of a window.

The children, of course,
were terribly upset.
"Poor Randolph!" they cried.

"Poor Randolph!"

"Poor Randolph!"

Oh yes,
and poor
Mrs Fritter.

17

By this time Mr Gaskitt
was in the supermarket
filling his trolley.

Horace was visiting
a friend who *seemed*
to be out.

Mrs Gaskitt
was also out …
of bed.

Hooray!

She was downstairs now in the sitting-room
watching TV, with a mug of hot chocolate
and a fried egg and pineapple –

 Pineapple?

– yes, pineapple
sandwich.

Meanwhile, somewhere
not very far away,
that pram was ...

...still whizzing along.

So, let's follow
the pram, shall we?
Here's a useful map.
It shows where the
pram has been so far
this morning and
where it's going.

Hm ... and here's
a big white van
with a ramp.
Now the pram
is being pushed
into the van.

MAP 1

SWIMMINGPOOL

CAF

SUPER

20

A

1   2   3   4   5

KEY:

‑ ‑ ‑ ‑ ‑ PRAM ROUTE

N

SCHOOL

Ha-ha!
What's going on here?

And look!
There's Horace
on a wall again,
outside his friend's
house.

Horace is a smart cat.
Well, *Horace* thinks
he is. He's thinking
now that if he sits
here for a while, his
friend will show up …
or something
interesting
might happen.

It probably will.

Chapter Three
Meet Mr Cruncher

Back at school Gus and Gloria
and the other children
were in the classroom
whispering about Randolph –

"Poor Randolph!"
"Poor Randolph!"

– and waiting for the
supply teacher. (Mrs Fritter
– nasty cuts and bruises –
had gone home in a taxi.)

Suddenly – Bang! –
the classroom
door flew open,
the windows rattled,
the floor shook …
and there he was.

Very tall.
Very wide.
With a great big
heavy bag.
And his name was,
MR CRUNCHER!

Mr Cruncher was a PE teacher,

a keep-fit fiend.

He had been in the army.

He had been in the navy.

He was a man of few words …

and he *loved* running.

Mr Blagg, the headmaster,

shook hands with Mr Cruncher –

Ooɐr!

– and wished he hadn't.

Mr Cruncher said, "Good morning, class!"

and the windows rattled again.

After that the lessons began.

During the morning
Mr Cruncher taught
reading, writing
and *running*.
But mostly running.

There were obstacle races

in the classroom, relay races

in the hall and laps and laps

And laps!

...on the school field.

By lunchtime
Gus and Gloria
and the others
had forgotten
Randolph,
and were puffing
and gasping
and sleeping even
... on the grass.

Meanwhile,
where's Horace?
He was on that wall
when we last saw him,
wasn't he?

But he's not there now.

Meanwhile also,
where's the pram?
Well, it's still
whizzing along – look! 
Down the road,
round the corner,
up the ramp …
and into the van.

It seems a bit odd,
that pram, doesn't it?
Let's take a closer look.

Let's see what
sort of *baby*
it's got in there.

Let's see, closer,

closer,

and closer…

Oh, no –

Miaow!

– they've got Horace!

Chapter Four
Have You Seen This Hamster?

By two o'clock that afternoon

trouble was brewing all over town.

There were cats missing,

and dogs missing,

gerbils,

guinea pigs – even goldfish!

Even budgerigars!

Even – well,

not just at this moment,

but fairly soon now – even *penguins!*

Yes, sad owners wandered
up and down the streets
whistling and calling,

"Here, Tibby!"

"Here, Marmaduke!"

"Here, Sweetie Pie!"

Some of them
put posters up,

HAVE YOU SEEN
THIS HAMSTER?

Some phoned
for the police.

Back at the school
the children heard
none of this.
All they knew about
was Randolph.

"Poor Randolph!"

HAVE YOU
SEEN THIS
HAMSTER?

call 014326578
with information

LOST.

All they cared about was
their sore feet.

For the literacy hour
Mr Cruncher had them
lifting heavy books.

In science
he had them lifting ...
each other!

And for music

  and art

    and home economics

  … he had them running.

When they got home,
Gus and Gloria sat on
their mother's bed
and told her
all about it.

"It's dreadful, Mum!"
"Our legs are
dropping off!"
"We're worn out!"

"Dear me," said Mrs Gaskitt,

or rather, "Drr ... mrr..."

She was eating a sandwich

at the time.

Yes, fried egg and

pineapple again.

Also, as you can see,

she was *in* bed again.

And it isn't even teatime.

Why *is* that?

Meanwhile, downstairs, Mr Gaskitt was cooking the children's tea, doing a bit of ironing and listening to the radio.

"THE MYSTERY OF THE MISSING PETS!"

yelled the radio.

"CATS AND DOGS VANISHING INTO THIN AIR!"

"POLICE BAFFLED!"

Mr Gaskitt folded a shirt
and put it on a pile.
He looked in the oven,
peered out of the window
and opened the
kitchen door.

"Hm." Mr Gaskitt gazed
thoughtfully into the garden
and rubbed his chin.

"Where's
Horace?"

MAP 2

So where *is* Horace?
Time, perhaps, for another useful map. This one shows where the van went with Horace in it. Ha-ha! Looks like they've taken him to the next town!

It also shows (it's a *very* useful map)

CINEMA

BUS

SOSSO

NEXT TOWN

GROCER

BOOKS

PET SHOP

BUS

N

B

A

1   2   3   4

KEY:
- - - - - VAN ROUTE
>>>>>> BUS ROUTE
• • • • RUNNING ROUTE

HOSPITAL

BUS 9

where the
Number 9
bus goes.
That could come
in handy.
And where,
tomorrow
morning bright
and early – actually,
it's going to rain –
Gus and Gloria
and the others
may very well,
if Mr Cruncher
gets his way,
may very well ...
be *running*.

Chapter Five
Honest Joe

That night Gus and Gloria did not sleep a wink.

All they could think about was,

Poor Horace!

They had walked the streets

and knocked on doors

and looked *everywhere* …

but couldn't find him.

Mr and Mrs Gaskitt
– look, she's out of bed! –
had driven all round the town
and *they* couldn't find him.

Meanwhile, in the *next* town …
in the back room of a pet shop
a large number of unhappy pets
were barking
and squealing
and twittering
and so on,
hoping to be let out.

Upstairs above the shop Honest Joe

was playing cards with his

honest mother and his

honest Uncle Sid.

Pet Shop? *Pet* Shop?

What's going on here?

And who's "Honest Joe"?

Well, Honest Joe –

it's time now you were told –

thinks of himself as a sort of *pet collector*.

He rescues animals, or so he says,

that are lost or strayed

and finds them

nice new cosy homes.

His mother and his uncle

help him in this work.

Usually they travel

round from town to town,

open a little shop for a while,

make a little money,

play a little cards …

and travel on.

Honest Joe means no harm.

He would not hurt a fly

– or so he says –

or a gerbil …

or a cat.

The worst he'd ever do

is put them in a shop –

Oh no, poor Horace! –

and sell them.

Chapter Six
The Great Escape

It was half past six in the morning.

Horace Gaskitt sat in the window

of Honest Joe's Pet Shop,

watching the world go by.

Horace was a brainy cat.

Well, Horace thought he was.

He was thinking now,

and had been thinking

since Honest Uncle Sid had grabbed him,

he was thinking now ... how to escape.

Meanwhile, in the window

next to Horace –

sat Randolph!

He was thinking of escaping too.

"What we need is a plan," said Horace.

"We could dig a tunnel, maybe –

or get a glass-cutter!"

"Hm." Randolph said nothing,

but rubbed his little chin.

Randolph, you see,

really *was* brainy.

He lived in a school after all.

Randolph was educated.

R A t
£ 2

Horace now was getting carried away.

"It could be great!" he cried. "Like that movie –

The Great Escape!

We could be famous –

on TV – wow!"

And he said (or rather yelled),

"We could make a rope ladder!

We could disguise ourselves!"

"No," said Randolph.

He was studying the

wire pen they were in.

"I've got a better idea.

Wake that guinea pig up."

The guinea pig's name was Maurice,

and he was not really asleep,

just fed up.

"It's hopeless," he groaned.

"We'll never get out."

"Yes, we will," said Randolph.

"Climb on Horace's back."

"What for?" said Maurice,

but he did it anyway.

And then – look at that!
Randolph, clever Randolph,
climbs up on Maurice's back
(on his head, actually),

RAt
£ 2

and

stretches

and

stretches

and

stretches up ...

to the catch ...

on the door ...

of the pen.

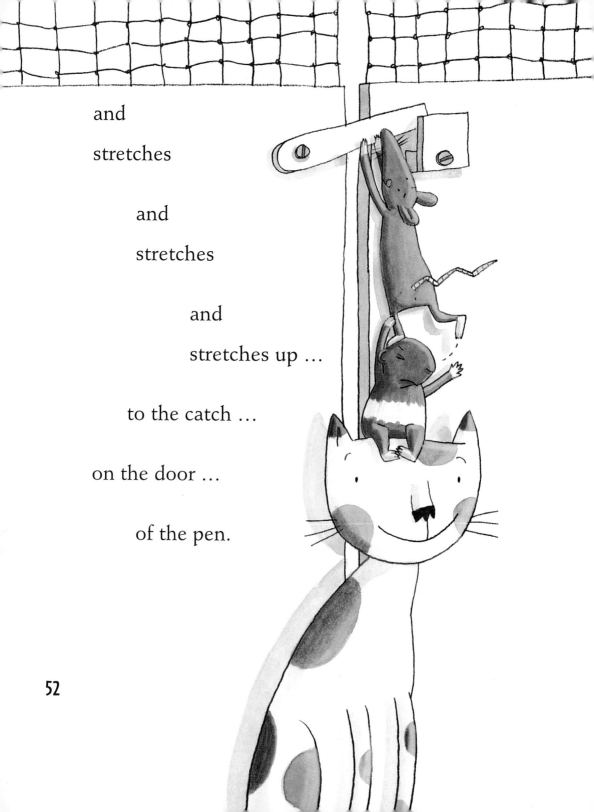

Chapter Seven
That Pram Again

Now the pace is quickening.

Now things are hotting up.

Now ... well, you get the idea.

Anyway, here's the TIMETABLE 👉

6:45

Horace, Maurice and Randolph tiptoe – Sh! – out of the
shop window.

7:30

Honest Joe, Mrs Gaskitt, Mrs Fritter and Mr Cruncher have their breakfasts. In different places, of course.

8:15

Honest Joe's mother loads the pram into the van and drives off with Honest Uncle Sid.

At the same time, Horace, Maurice and Randolph creep out through the open door and run off down the street.

8:55

Gus and Gloria and the others get changed for their cross-country run.

The rain begins to fall.
Five minutes later, Mrs
Fritter falls too,

*Poor
Mrs Fritter!*

tripping up over a rug on
her way to the bathroom.

9:15

Uncle Sid takes
his "baby"
for a stroll in
the *zoo*.

The Number 9 bus,
meanwhile, leaves Fish
Street – eight minutes late.

9:30

Mrs Gaskitt sits up in bed. She
has a funny look on her face.
Can you see? She looks happy
and sad at the same time.

Why is that?

9:45

Mr Cruncher
and his class
are off –
"Puff, gasp!"
– on their run.

At the same time, down a little
street at the back of the zoo –
look, here it comes! – that pram
again, with Honest Uncle Sid

… just *whizzing* along.

Chapter Eight
Clever Randolph!

Horace, Maurice and Randolph

were hiding behind a litter bin

next to a bus shelter.

Randolph was thoughtful.

Maurice was gloomy.

And Horace …

was getting carried away.

"It's like in that movie!" he cried.

"*The Incredible Journey* – where these pets

travel thousands and thousands of miles

to get back home!"

"Was one of them a guinea pig?" said Maurice.

"Can't remember," said Horace.

"Anyway, we could do that!
Hide out in a barn –
follow the stars
at night …
have adventures."

But Randolph
only coughed
and rubbed his
little chin.
"No," he said.
"I've got a
better idea."

LoSt.

Meanwhile, outside the zoo,

Honest Uncle Sid was whizzing along

with a pramful of penguins.

Yes – penguins!

He was supposed to get *parrots*

but Uncle Sid had always

wanted a penguin.

Or two.

Or eight.

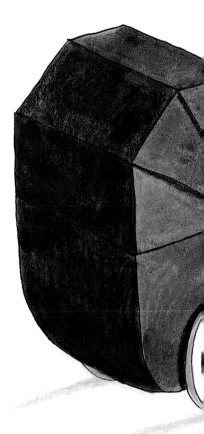

Anyway, there he was,

whizzing along,

when who should

he spy outside the scout hut

but a little tiny tied-up spotted dozy … dog.

"Room for one more!"
cried Uncle Sid.
And he grabbed up
the little dog and
was just pushing him
in with the penguins,
when …

round the corner came

Gus and Gloria and

Tracey and Billy and a few others.

Meanwhile also,

Goodness me!

Mr and Mrs Gaskitt were driving by.

They spotted Gus and Gloria and waved ...

but couldn't stop. Mr Gaskitt was

taking Mrs Gaskitt – Oh, no! –

to the hospital.

What's wrong?

Is she poorly?

She doesn't look poorly.

Meanwhile *also*, the
Number 9 bus was...
But things are getting
a bit complicated,
don't you think?

Perhaps we
could do with ...

MAP 3

one more map.

See – there's the pram with the van parked round the corner.

There's Gus and Gloria and the others, including Mr Cruncher.

There's Mr and Mrs Gaskitt in their car.

There's the Number 9 bus.

POLICE

PO

UPER

BAKER

NEXT TOWN

SWIMMING POOL

A

1   2   3   4   5

And there –
can you see? –
upstairs on the bus,
on the front seat,
side by side,
cosy, safe and
sharing a
bag of crisps
they've found …

there's Horace,
and Maurice
and …
clever
Randolph.

63

Chapter Nine
Running Like the Wind

But what happened

next, you'll say.

Hm ... well,

let's see.

      pram. (That

        little dozy

        dog was wide

      awake now.)

    Like a rocket

he went,

round the

  corner,

Uncle Sid

whizzed off

with his once

more barking

down

the street,

up the ramp,

into the van ...

and away.

And after him
came Gus
and Gloria
and Billy
and Tracey.
And Marigold
and Mary
and Tom
and Rupert
and Buster
and Polly
and
Esmeralda
and
Mr Cruncher …
and a few others.

So the race
began. The race?
Race? Between
a van and children?
Yes – and it was much
closer than you'd think.
See – the children
were young, strong,
and ran like the wind.
Mr Cruncher was
proud of them.

65

Meanwhile, the van was old, stolen and had failed its MOT.

So what with traffic-lights and zebra crossings and so on, Gus and Gloria

and the others

kept up with it ...

down this road,

down that,

up this hill,

over that bridge ...

all the way to

the next town.

All the way, in fact, to *Honest Joe's.*

Honest Joe, meanwhile,
was hard at work serving
a customer.

Suddenly in burst his
honest mother, his honest
uncle, a grumpy little
barking dog,
four or five penguins –
"Penguins!" cried Joe.
"Where's the parrots?" –
and a whole classful
of hot and
steaming …

"KIDS!"

Not to mention
Mr Cruncher.

Then the *battle* began.
Well, it wasn't
much of a battle.
Honest Joe's mother
tried to sneak off,
but tripped up
over a penguin
and was sat on by
some of the bigger girls.
And the penguin.

Honest
Joe punched
Mr Cruncher in
the tummy –
Ooer!
– and wished
he hadn't.

Honest Uncle Sid
looked at the odds,
shrugged his
shoulders and
surrendered.

Meanwhile, at the hospital,

Mrs Gaskitt was in bed *again*.

A doctor with a stethoscope

was listening to *her* tummy.

Hm. What's going on here?

Let's have a listen too.

Shall we?

Sh…

"Where am I?

What's happening?

It's very dark in here.

I could just eat a doughnut.

Oh – here we go!

It's getting lighter...

Where? Where... Waaaa!"

So there we are. (Did you guess?)

At half past one in the afternoon

on a Wednesday

in September

Mrs Gaskitt (and Mr Gaskitt too)

had – their – baby.

Little Gary Gaskitt:
brown hair
blue eyes
7lb 12oz

Congratulations!

Chapter Ten
The Final Timetable

Now the pace is slowing.

Now things are winding down.

Now ... well, you get the idea.

Anyway, here's the final

TIMETABLE

1:30

Little Gary Gaskitt arrives.

1:45

The police arrive (not at the
hospital, though) and load
Honest Joe and his gang
into a van.

The police are happy.
They have captured some
dangerous criminals –
and got their
dog back.

Hello,
Sweetie Pie

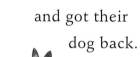

2:15

Meanwhile, Gus and
Gloria and the other
children are sad.
All these rescued pets, but
where's Horace? Where's
Randolph? And where (if
they'd only ever heard of
him), where's Maurice?

2:40

The children arrive ...
back at the school.
Hooray!

Hooray!

Hooray!

There they are!

4:00

In the police cell Honest Joe and his mother play a little cards ...

and win a little money.

5:30

Mrs Fritter watches TV and thinks of going back to school.

Mr Cruncher goes off for an early evening run with his girlfriend.

At the same time, Mr Gaskitt drives Gus and Gloria and Horace to the hospital ... for the happy ending.

And the happy beginning!

Chapter Eleven
Meanwhile...

One week later the Gaskitts –

all five of them –

were at home sitting

side by side on the sofa.

All except little Gary.

He was in his carrycot.

Anyway,

there they were

drinking coffee,

eating cake

and sticking photos

of Gary in

the family album.

There was a photo of Gary –

aged one hour,

a photo of Gary –

aged one day,

a photo of Gary –

aged two days ...

and so on.

Meanwhile, little Gary himself just lies there
in his cot and watches the world go by.

Gary Gaskitt is a clever baby.
(Well, Mrs Gaskitt thinks he is.)
He's thinking now
that if he lies there
long enough, something –

Yawn!

– something
interesting
might happen.

It probably will.

Bye-bye!